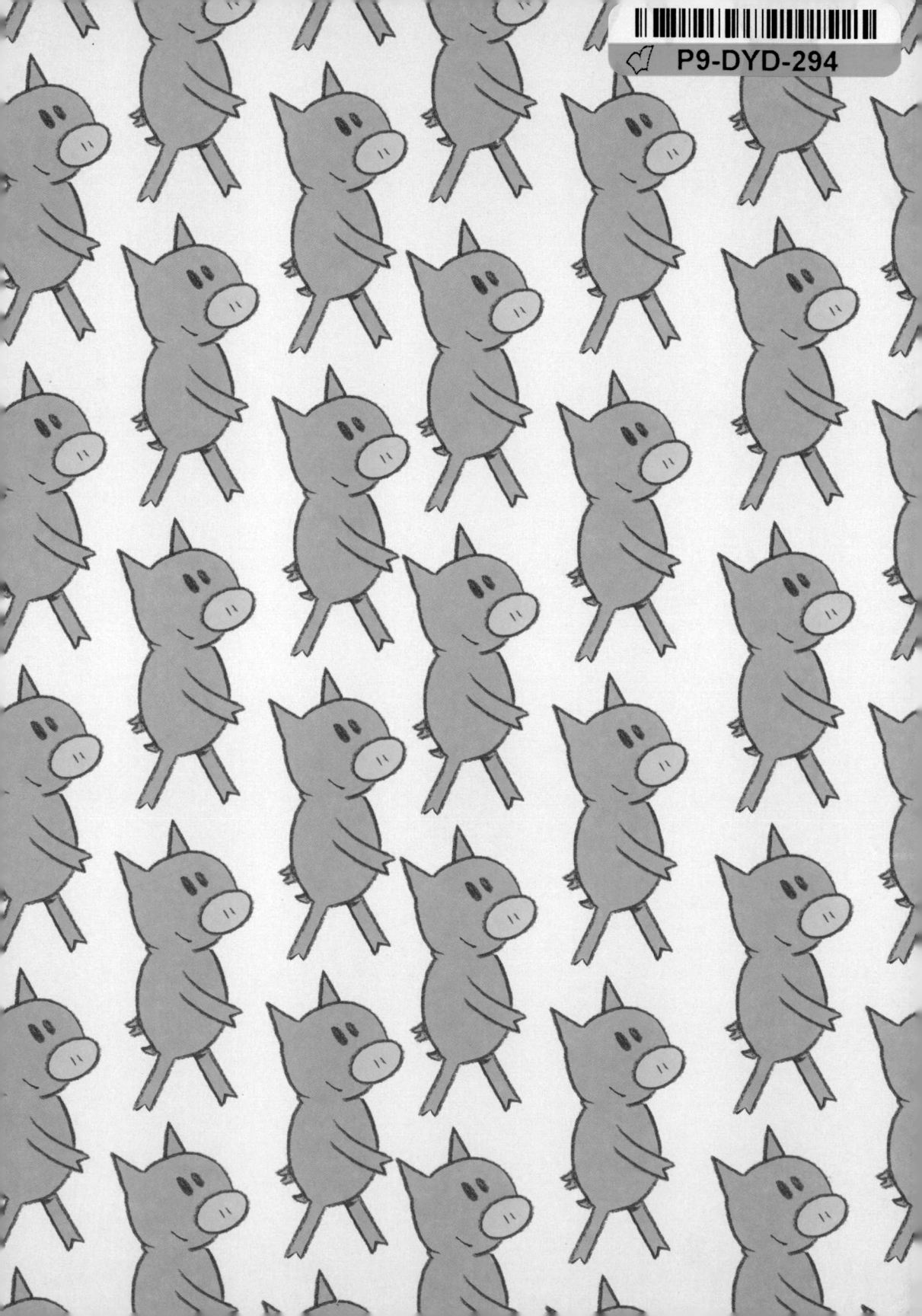

P9-DYD-294

To Toshi and Jaxson

Text and illustrations copyright © 2010 by Mo Willems

All rights reserved. Published by Hyperion Books for Children, an imprint of Disney Book Group. No part of this book may be reproduced or transmitted in any form or by any means, electronic or mechanical, including photocopying, recording, or by any information storage and retrieval system, without written permission from the publisher.
For information address Hyperion Books for Children, 114 Fifth Avenue, New York, New York 10011-5690.
Printed in Singapore
Reinforced binding
First Edition
10 9 8 7 6 5 4 3
F850-6835-5-10159

Library of Congress Cataloging-in-Publication Data on file.
ISBN: 978-1-4231-1990-6

Visit www.hyperionbooksforchildren.com and www.pigeonpresents.com

I Am Going!

By Mo Willems

An ELEPHANT & PIGGIE Book

Hyperion Books for Children/*New York*
AN IMPRINT OF DISNEY BOOK GROUP

This is a
good day.

Just like yesterday.

Yes!
Yesterday was a good day, too.

Well, I am going.

You are *going*?!

You are going away?!

Yes.

You cannot go!

You must not go!

I WILL NOT
LET YOU GO!!!

POP!

I am going.

PIG

GIE!

What about me?

Who will I skip with?

Who will I play Ping-Pong with?

Who will I wear
a silly hat with?

WHO WILL I SKIP AND PLAY PING-PONG IN A SILLY HAT WITH?!?!

I am sorry, Gerald.

But, I am going.

Fine.

Then *I* will go, too!

Watch me go!

I am going!

Look at me go!

Have fun.

WAIT!
Go later!

Go tomorrow!

Go next week!

Go next month!

GO NEXT YEAR!!!

I am
going now.

NOW!?!

Why,
Piggie?

Why? Why?
Why? Why?
Why? Why?
Why? Why?
Why? Why?
Why? Why?
Why? Why?
Why? Why?

Why? *Why?*
Why? Why?
Why? *Why?*
Why? Why?
Why? *Why?*
Why? Why?
Why? *Why?*
Why? Why
Why? *Why*

Why?

It is lunchtime, Gerald.

Lunchtime?

I am going to eat lunch.

You are going to eat lunch?
Yes.

Oh.

Piggie?

Yes,
Gerald?

Is it a
big lunch?

This is a good day.

Just like yesterday...

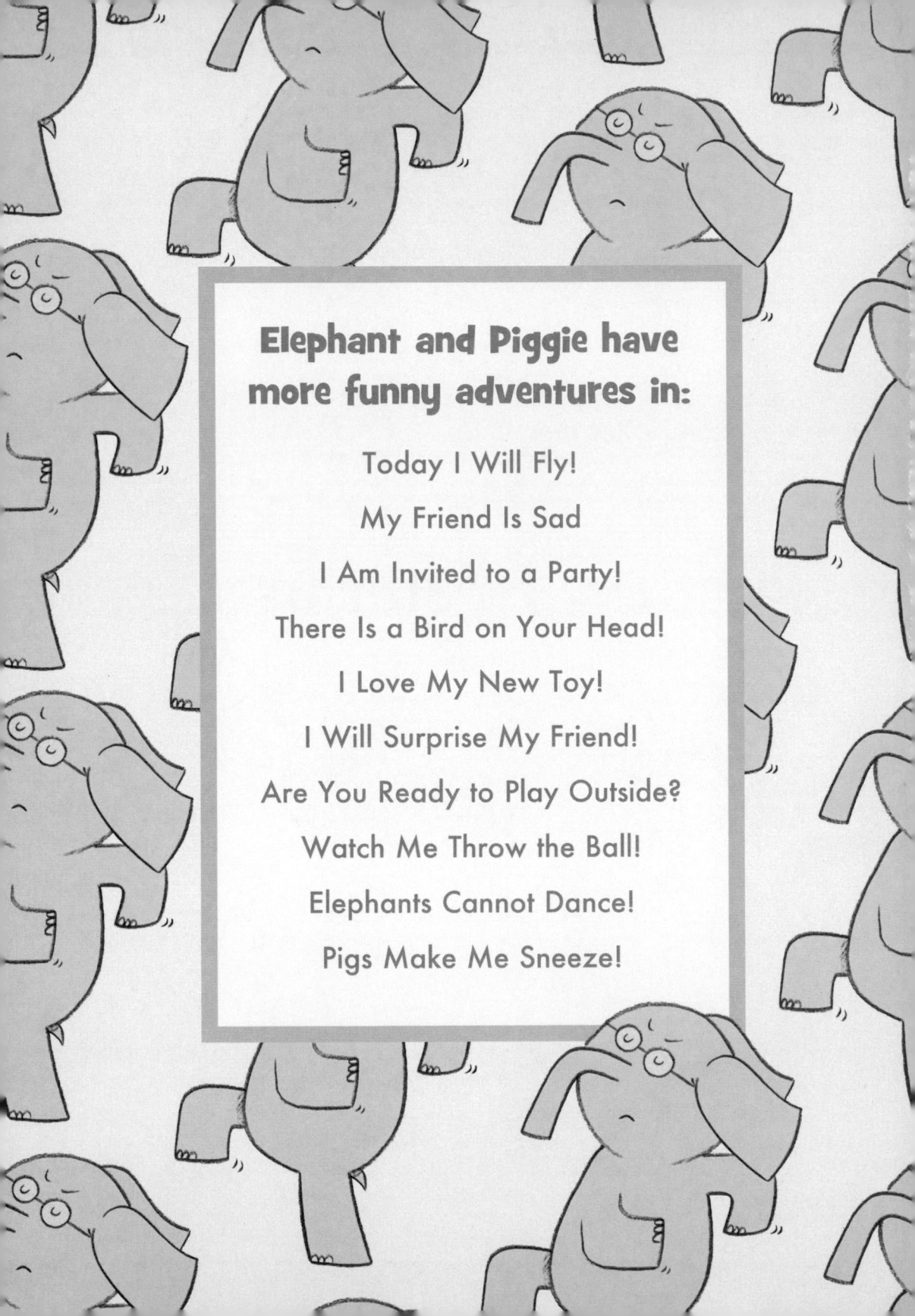

Elephant and Piggie have more funny adventures in:

Today I Will Fly!

My Friend Is Sad

I Am Invited to a Party!

There Is a Bird on Your Head!

I Love My New Toy!

I Will Surprise My Friend!

Are You Ready to Play Outside?

Watch Me Throw the Ball!

Elephants Cannot Dance!

Pigs Make Me Sneeze!